Jane's Journal

Best wishes
Margaret Ball

Jane's Journal

By

Margaret Ball

Blackie & Co
Publishers Ltd

A BLACKIE & CO PUBLISHERS PAPERBACK

First published in 2003

A CIP catalogue record for this title is
available from the British Library

ISBN 1-903138-78-7

**Blackie & Co Publishers Ltd
107-111 Fleet Street
LONDON EC4A 2AB**

To My Daughter Juliet
1952 - 1986

October 7 1546

Yesterday was the ninth anniversary of my birth. My father, the Duke of Suffolk, has sent me a chestnut mare. I shall call her Bella, because she is so beautiful. My mother gave me this leather-bound journal and told me I must record all the important events of my life. I fear there will be but few entries, for life here at Chelsea is uneventful. My days pass in study, needlework and music.

Dear Edward gave me a silver chain with an ivory cross. Elizabeth sewed a kerchief for me, which she embroidered herself. This indeed was a labour of love, for she does not care for needlework. I trow she mislikes any pastime which compels her to sit still for long.

She is four years older than I am and quite grown-up. Although she and Edward have the same father, they are very different. Elizabeth is so robust and Edward so delicate. He does not remember his mother, who died when he was born. Sometimes I wonder whether Elizabeth remembers hers, for she was only three years old when Anne Boleyn went to the block. We never speak of it.

Queen Katharine has been a kind stepmother to them both and a good friend to me. Sometimes she looks sad. Elizabeth says it is because has no child. King Henry would like a second son. I will say a prayer for her that she might be fruitful.

Our tutor, John Cheke, is pleased with my work and I am content. It was a happy day for me when I was brought here to study with Edward and Elizabeth. Mr Aylmer, who was my tutor at Bradgate, was overmuch strict. Two days before I left he caned me on both palms because there were two errors in my translation from Plato.

Phoebe bathed my hands with witch hazel. Phoebe Wylliams is my maid. She has been with me since I was four years old, and has become both companion and friend. Her family live in a little seaport called Topsham, in Devonshire. It lies on the Exe estuary and looks out across the water towards Powderham Castle, the home of the Courtenays, Earls of Devon. Phoebe says, 'Tis not quite sea, yet more than river. Tis the last place the Good Lord made, and he didn't stop to finish it or we would have had sand, not mud.' She often speaks of her family. Her father was drowned at sea. Her mother and her sister Dorcas live with an uncle, Robert Yeandall, who is vicar of the parish of St Margaret in Topsham.

Phoebe is devoted to me. When Mr Aylmer used to beat me and lock me in my room for punishment, I trow Phoebe suffered more than I did. Sometimes he would make me stand at the lectern for nigh on two hours. I was thankful when he went back to Oxford.

I have studied Latin and Greek since I was five years old, and I am also studying French and Spanish. Next year I am to study Hebrew. Edward says I have a flair for languages. In truth I do not find study tedious, and I try to be good. It is not always easy to please. My solace comes from prayer. On my knees in the chapel I come to peace and a quiet mind. God never fails me.

October 14 1546

Today our tutor John Cheke set us all to study the tragedies of Sophocles. While we were thus occupied, King Henry arrived in the schoolroom unannounced. He was limping heavily. He asked John Cheke if we were making good progress and seemed pleased with his replies. Then he spoke to each of us in turn. I expressed the hope that his leg was less painful today. He has said that I may call him 'uncle' though in truth I am but his great-niece, being the granddaughter of his sister Mary, and great granddaughter of Henry the Seventh.

He questioned me in Latin and seemed pleased with my answers. He said I was a diligent scholar. I know he sets a great store by learning, and it pleases him that Queen Katharine can both read and write fluent Latin.

He asked me if I thought Edward looked well. I said I did, though methinks I lied. Dear Edward. I would he were stronger. Yesterday we walked in the garden together. He admired my dress. It was my favourite gown of moss green velvet. He said it was his dearest wish that when he became king we two should be married. I reminded him that kings may not always marry where they will, but he swore that he would have no other wife. He has spoken of this to his uncle, Thomas Seymour, who approves wholeheartedly. Tomorrow we shall ride together. We find much pleasure in each other's company.

October 15 1546

Our excursion yesterday was a brief one. Edward had a fit of coughing which was so severe that he could barely sit his horse. We turned back at once. He looked very pale and said he would lie down. I told the groom not to unsaddle Bella but to ride her for an hour, for she was restive and needed exercise. Then I sought out Queen Katharine. She went at once to Edward. She is a capable nurse, for she cared for two ailing husbands before she married the King. He will allow no-one else to dress his leg. He says she has gentle hands. She changes his bandages three times a day. She told me he was often in great pain. I am sorry for that.

Phoebe, who is ever eager to be the first with news, told me that Martin Luther has died. I know that the queen is secretly reading one of his books, *The Babylonian Captivity of the Church*. She became interested in the New Religion while she was married to her second husband, Lord Latimer, though he was a Catholic.

Luther's teachings have spread far and wide. He holds that the Scriptures contain all that is necessary for salvation, which comes by faith alone. Many are reading the forbidden books which are being smuggled into the country. In Billingsgate a press was seized, which had been printing forbidden pamphlets. The printers were thrown into prison. All books on the New Religion, including Tyndale's translation, have been banned. Many Protestants have emigrated to France and the Rhineland, where they are more tolerant, and allow people to worship God in their own way.

October 31 1546

I was crossing the courtyard on my way to see Elizabeth, when I encountered Phoebe. She told me that the old crone Anne Dowe was in the kitchen telling fortunes. She has told Phoebe that she will marry, but not for many years yet, and then to a man much older than she is. Phoebe urged me to let Anne Dowe read my palm. Elizabeth joined us and was eager to have her fortune told. When I said I did not think it right to try and look into the future, Elizabeth laughed and said it was but a game. She sent Phoebe to fetch Anne Dowe.

The old crone peered into Elizabeth's palm and muttered so low that we could scarcely hear her words. She said that Elizabeth would have a long life and riches and all things her heart desired, 'save one.' Then she took my hand. She said not a word. I asked her if I too should have a long life, but without answering she dropped my hand and hurried away.

Elizabeth said that Anne Dowe is *non compos mentis*, but she must have been pleased with her fortune, for she sent Phoebe after the old woman with a coin.

December 2 1546

It gives me great pleasure to write down my thoughts in this journal. My great-grandfather, Henry the Seventh, also kept a journal. Unfortunately his pet monkey tore it to pieces, which vexed him greatly.

Queen Katharine sat and talked with us today. She looked pale and tired. She said the King's leg does not improve and gives him great pain. The fistula will not heal. She nurses him so patiently. We all love her.

The King makes no secret of his displeasure because she has not given him a son. Hans Holbein is painting a family portrait but the King will not allow Katharine to be included. He sits in the centre, with Edward beside him and Mary and Elizabeth on either side. He has ordered Holbein to paint in Jane Seymour, for he said she was the only wife who had given him a son. I can imagine how this must have hurt the Queen. She must be fearful. Is it another sign that the King is losing patience with her because she has not borne him a son? In truth it is not always a happy thing to be a queen.

We were all greatly cheered when Sir Thomas Seymour arrived. He is Edward's favourite uncle and always makes us merry. As soon as he arrived the Queen excused herself and left immediately. Sir Thomas teased Elizabeth outrageously and she revelled in it, while feigning disapproval. When he left he gave Edward a purse of coin. Elizabeth asked me if I did not think him handsome and I had to confess that I did.

December 3 1546

Edward and I were in the schoolroom when Elizabeth told us the news. The Earl of Surrey has been arrested for treason. He was charged with the improper use of Royal Arms. They say he believes the king has not long to live, and he has amended his coat of arms.

By displaying the Royal Arms in the first quarter he hopes to draw attention to his claim to be descended from Edward the Confessor. One can imagine King Henry's fury when he learned of it. By opening admitting ambitions towards the throne, the Earl has signed his own death warrant. His father, the Duke of Norfolk, warned him many times, '*Indignatio principis mors est*,' the anger of the prince is death, but he heeded it not.

Later, as we fed the swans beside the Long Pond, Elizabeth said the he was reckless and had allowed his ambition to overcome common sense. She left us to go to her music lesson. Edward and I sat in the summerhouse and spoke of many things. He said he hoped we would always be together. I believe we should be happy, for we never disagree and I love him truly. By mutual consent we do not speak of this when Elizabeth is present. She likes to point out that Edward and I are related, though we are but second cousins. I believe she may be jealous because Edward spends so much time with me.

December 10 1546

A cold day, but the sun shone. Edward and I were to ride in the forest but he said he was too weary to ride. He looked tired and pale and coughed a good deal. I left him lying down in a darkened room. His health causes much anxiety to those who love him.

When I returned to the schoolroom I found Elizabeth walking restlessly up and down. She said she had been ordered to return to Hatfield with her governess. She was not pleased and sulked for the rest of the day. I know she is thinking that when Sir Thomas comes again she will not be here.

Phoebe brought a message from the Queen. It seems that the King has a fever and the Queen is concerned. She is so tenderhearted. She it was who persuaded the King to bring Mary and Elizabeth to court.

December 19 1546

My family has always been Protestant. There are things in the Catholic religion which I cannot comprehend: they maintain that during the Communion the bread actually becomes the Body of Christ and the wine becomes his blood. How can this be? Bread is bread and wine is wine. Surely we take these in remembrance of Him. Did He not say to His disciples, 'Do this in remembrance of me?' This is my belief. A man must worship according to his conscience. To obey the Ten Commandments, that is the important thing, for of a surety they are the best set of rules ever set down for man's guidance.

December 31 1546

Christmas passed quietly this year and without the usual boisterous revels. Edward is still ailing, and King Henry, all other cures having failed, has been driven to having his leg cauterized. This is a painful remedy, but one which often proves efficacious.

Mary, Elizabeth and I went to Greenwich. The Queen was reluctant to go because she was anxious about the King's health, but eventually she was persuaded. The King's leg shows no sign of healing and Edward coughs persistently.

While we were at Greenwich the Queen lent me a copy of Sir Thomas More's *Utopia*. I found it most interesting. It is a devout book, full of ideals and new ideas, though somewhat puritanical. He asserts that the greatest good for the individual is to seek the good of all. I would like to read his book *Dialogue of Comfort* when the Queen will lend it to me.

My grandfather, the late Duke of Suffolk, was at the final trial of Sir Thomas More, when the jury condemned him. Sir Thomas was a good man, a man of great integrity. He could have saved his life by speaking a few words, but his conscience would not allow it. Even his beloved daughter Margaret could not persuade him to change his mind.

Erasmus, who was his friend, called him 'a man for all seasons.'

January 10 1547

We returned from Greenwich to good news. It seems the King's leg is much better. The Queen went to him at once. He welcomed her, saying that no - one could bandage his leg as well as she could. He was plainly glad to see her and she was relieved to find him a little improved. She played chess with him and as usual he won. This put him in a merry mood.

The musicians played a new galliard which he had composed, and we congratulated him in all sincerity, for it was a goodly tune.

Three of the Dudley brothers are at court. Robert is by far the most handsome. By comparison Ambrose and Guildford seem dull. Robert is married to an heiress, Amy Robsart, who is sixteen years old and very pretty. Their home is Hemsley Manor, near Yarmouth, though Robert is seldom there. He prefers to spend much time at court. Amy remains in the country. It is said that his father disapproved of the match, but Robert is wilful and would have his way.

January 21 1547

Today the Earl of Surrey was executed for treason. He was an ambitious man and fatally indiscreet. He boasted that he had Plantagenet blood in his veins and was descended from Edward the Confessor. It is common knowledge that he has included the Royal Arms on his own coat of arms, and has had the leopards of England carved on a panel at Kenninghall. His latest indiscretion was to state that his father should by right become regent upon the King's death.

After he was arrested and taken to the Tower he tried to escape by climbing down the privy shaft, but he was caught.

At his trial he was arrogant to the last. He stated that the trial was a farce, for, he said, 'They always find the fallen guilty.'

His father, the Duke of Norfolk, is also a prisoner in the Tower. Doubtless he will soon suffer the same fate as his son.

January 22 1547

After the execution yesterday morning, strange rumours were being bruited abroad. A sudden rumbling was heard after the Earl of Surrey died. Some said it was an earthquake, some thought great guns were being fired. Others said it sounded like a troop of horses stampeding. People fell to the earth with fear, and many ran away affrighted.

January 28 1547

The bells are tolling. There is a hush over the palace. King Henry died at two of the clock this morning. He had been confined to his bed for the past two weeks. At the end he sent for the Queen. She approached the bed but could not speak for weeping.

The King had asked to be buried with Queen Jane, near the altar in Saint George's Chapel at Windsor. He was fifty-five years old and had reigned for nearly thirty-eight years.

Archbishop Cranmer was sent for but the King could not speak to him. The Archbishop held his hand and the King pressed it. Shortly after this he died.

Lord Hertford left at once for Ashridge to tell Edward that he was king. Edward burst into tears. Elizabeth told me this for she was with him. He has been taken to the Royal apartments in the Tower.

February 2 1547

We missed Edward in the schoolroom today. We shall not see him until his coronation, which is to take place on the twenty-fifth of February. Elizabeth is excited. She has been measured for new robes.

The Queen sat with us this morning. While we studied she worked at her tapestry. When she left Elizabeth told me she was now a very wealthy lady. She has had handsome provision made for her in the King's will, and still retains fortunes from her two previous husbands.

I searched for Phoebe in vain this morning. When I asked her where she had been she said she had been to the hives to tell the bees that King Henry was dead.

February 8 1547

In every church in England the bells are tolling for the passing of the King, and they are celebrating a Requiem Mass in Latin.

Although the King made himself head of the Church in England, the services and ritual have remained the same. The only difference is that the King is now head of the Church and not the Pope. We are all in mourning. The funeral is to take place next week. The King lies in state in the chapel of Whitehall.

The Queen must be feeling both sorrow and relief. The King's moods were becoming ever more unpredictable. In his cell in the Tower Norfolk must be thanking heaven for his deliverance. He has escaped death, for the King had not signed his death warrant.

February 15 1547

Yesterday the King was buried in St George's Chapel at Windsor, beside Jane Seymour, the mother of his son. The funeral procession was four miles long. In the chapel Bishop Gardiner preached a sermon on the text ' Blessed are the dead which die in the Lord' and the enormous coffin was lowered into the grave by sixteen Yeomen of the Guard, using a vice. Then they broke their staves of office over their heads and threw them down onto the coffin. Deo Profundis was said and the pit was covered with planks.

Edward was not present, as is customary. I stood beside the Queen. As the pit was being covered she swayed and leaned on me. I took her arm and led her outside. The heavens were overcast and dark clouds scudded across the sky. As we stood there a heavy rain began to fall.

I tried to imagine what thoughts must be going through her mind. She would be sad, for she had a genuine affection for the late King, but mingled with that sadness there must surely be relief. The shadow which had hung over her has gone. Never again will she hear the words which have haunted her for the past four years, 'I must have sons.' Of a surety freedom must be very sweet to her.

February 19 1547

Amid scenes of great splendour Edward was crowned today. He wore a gold-embroidered gown of silver cloth and wore a velvet cap trimmed with diamonds and pearls. His horse was caparisoned with crimson satin, and he rode under a canopy carried by six mounted noblemen. He looked serious and very pale.

The ceremony was long and tiring. When it was all over the people cried, 'God save the King!' They feel safe because Edward is devoted to the Reformed Faith. They do not want the Spanish Inquisition in England.

I hoped Edward would be able to rest after the ceremony, but Lord Hertford had arranged a celebration supper at Seymour Place, which we all had to attend. The Queen took me aside. She told me that although I am too young to be a maid of honour she wishes me to be her companion. She said it pleases her to have me near her.

Everything has changed. I fear I shall see little of Edward in the days ahead. Sometimes I recall how we used to speak of marriage, but 'twas idle talk. Kings may not marry where they will. I have decided I shall never marry, for I cannot imagine loving anyone else.

March 2 1547

I have received a short letter from Edward. He has been acknowledged Supreme Head of the Church. He writes with great sadness of the death of his father, but says that his parents are now united in Heaven. He says he misses me now that I am no longer at court, but hopes to see me ere long.

He has made John Dudley Earl of Warwick. Lord Hertford has been named Lord Protector, and created Duke of Somerset. His brother, Sir Thomas Seymour, has been created Lord Sudeley and Lord High Admiral of the Fleet. Edward has given him Sudeley Castle in Gloucestershire.

Edward tells me that he has a present for me but he will not tell me what it is. It is to be a surprise.

March 19 1547

Edward's present has arrived. It is a tiny Maltese Spaniel. I have named her Dulcia. She is so pretty. She sits quietly in my lap while I read or do my embroidery. Phoebe, who does not like dogs, calls her a scrap and says she will be forever underfoot.

April 12 1547

Elizabeth has been to see me. She asked me to dismiss Phoebe so that we could speak privately. She enquired whether Lord Sudeley had been to visit the Queen recently. I told her no. Then she revealed that he had spoken to her of marriage. She told him she was too young, being but fourteen years of age. He replied that this was a condition which time would mend. Elizabeth is shrewd. She would not commit herself, yet I know she finds him attractive.

I confess I am surprised at his behaviour. I had thought he looked towards the Queen, for it is well-known they were all but betrothed when King Henry chose her for his sixth wife. I fear Lord Sudeley is ambitious and will marry where it best furthers his own interests. Albeit he is treading on dangerous ground. As for Elizabeth, she knows well that the Council would never allow such a marriage.

April 15 1547

I spent the afternoon with Queen Katharine and Elizabeth. I worked at my petit point. Elizabeth is sewing a shirt for Edward. She paused often to speak of recent events and also I trow because she finds plain sewing tedious.

When the Queen left us to visit Edward, who has a cold, Elizabeth spoke of the latest gossip. It seems that Lord Sudeley has been seen entering the Queen's apartments after dark and not leaving until dawn.

I can scarcely credit it. I know the Queen admires him and speaks fairly of him, but I was sure his eye was on Elizabeth. He is a bold man. I would I could warn the Queen that his visits have been observed. Elizabeth thinks we should say nothing and await events. She is out of humour today because she cannot be with Edward.

She told me that John Dudley, Earl of Warwick, has been made Duke of Northumberland. Never before has anyone, other than royalty assumed the title of duke.

May 12 1547

The Queen summoned me. She said she trusted me and knew that I could be discreet. Then she revealed that she and Lord Sudeley were married two days ago. She did not want it made known immediately, for it is only four months since King Henry died. She fears folk will say she has married in unseemly haste. She spoke of her marvellous new-found happiness. She said she had always loved Thomas. He had asked her to marry him in 1543 but she had delayed too long and the King's eye had fallen upon her. From that time onwards she and Thomas had not dared to exchange a glance. She has been three times a widow. All her husbands were chosen for her. This time she was determined to choose for herself.

I am truly glad for her. She deserves to be happy. She has loved Thomas Seymour long and faithfully. I hope he will be worthy of her. I cannot account for my distrust of him. It is true there have been rumours of his philandering, but there is always gossip at court. Edward clearly admires him and Elizabeth is never happier than when he is teasing her and she is flirting with him. Katharine thinks he is perfect. Why then do I have these doubts about him? Mayhap it is because Katharine is very dear to me and I am concerned for her happiness.

May 13 1547

Katharine and Thomas are to honeymoon at Sudeley Castle. I am to go with them. They told me that Edward was consulted before the wedding and wholeheartedly approved of the match, for he loves them both. I fear Elizabeth will not be pleased. It was not so long ago that Thomas proposed marriage to her. Mayhap it was in jest. I would like to think so.

Mary has written expressing her displeasure. She thinks the marriage is too soon after her father's death. Katharine's brother-in-law, the Protector, is not pleased either. His wife Anne has always been jealous of Katharine. It would seem that this sudden marriage does not meet with universal approval.

Katharine is so much in love that she cares for none of the criticism. She has been in love with Thomas for many years and now at last he is her husband, and she is truly happy.

May 28 1547

The plague has broken out again. Katharine says it is dangerous to remain in Chelsea and we are to move to Hanworth to avoid infection. Elizabeth is to go with us. While we are away the privies will be emptied and the house sweetened.

My sister Catherine paid me a visit yesterday. She asked me if Katharine was happy in her marriage. She has heard rumours about Thomas and Elizabeth. He has been seen teasing and tickling her, and even goes to her bedchamber before she has risen. Her maid, Kat Ashley, has warned him that such behaviour will give rise to gossip. Elizabeth does not seem to care. I trow she has always had a secret liking for Thomas. Doubtless she believes that it is safe to flirt with him now that he is safely married.

I told Catherine that I hope Katharine will not be hurt by these rumours. She assured me that she is often present on these occasions and appears to treat it all as a harmless game. I like it not.

June 20 1547

My father has informed me that I am to become the ward of Thomas and Katharine. I am to live with them. Tomorrow Phoebe and I will move to their favourite house at Hanworth. This is indeed good news. I have grown very fond of Katharine and we have become close friends. She is so happy in her marriage and her love for Thomas is plain to see. She says it would be a good thing if Edward and I were to marry. She knows we are devoted to each other.

I have packed my books and Phoebe has packed my clothes, prattling happily the while. She is as pleased as I am at this change in our lives.

June 29 1547

Thomas has asked permission for Elizabeth to join our household and Edward has agreed. She and Katherine have always been on good terms and Katharine is like a mother to her, and Thomas is a favourite with everyone. It gave Edward great pleasure to create him Lord Sudeley and to give him Sudeley Castle in the heart of the beautiful Gloucestershire country – side.

Katharine looks so contented these days. She adores Thomas and her happiness is plain to see. In one year she has passed from shadow into sunlight.

A year ago King Henry was losing patience because there was no sign of a son.

Katharine must have been fearful, remembering the fate of Anne Boleyn and Catherine Howard. If the king had not died, who knows what fate might have befallen her? She must now feel herself doubly blessed.

July 3 1547

This morning I stood at the casement admiring the gardens. The roses are beautiful. The gardeners were clipping the neat yew hedges. Suddenly I heard voices and Elizabeth came into view. She was wearing a black velvet dress which I had never seen before. It was low cut and fitted closely to her body. She was followed by Thomas and Katharine. They were all laughing. I could not hear what they were saying.

Suddenly Thomas tugged at Elizabeth's skirt. She pulled away, and as she did so the dress split at the seams. He tugged at it a second time and it fell away from her shoulders. For a moment she stood there exposed in her petticoats, then laughing she ran across the grass and into the house.

It appeared to cause Thomas great amusement, yet I sensed that Katharine was uneasy. She loves Thomas so much that she cannot think ill of aught that he does. Mayhap she blames Elizabeth who of a surety does nothing to discourage him.

July 15 1547

Katharine was melancholy today. I ventured to ask if aught was amiss. She told me she was remembering her friend Anne Askew, who was burned as a heretic one year ago on this day. Anne was racked unmercifully but she steadfastly refused to incriminate her friends. She was offered pardon if she would recant, but she refused and said that she had not come there to deny her Master.

We spoke of the time last year when Katharine herself was in great danger. Chancellor Wriothesley was anxious to implicate her. He told the King that she was reading forbidden books and was interested in the New Religion. He had chosen an opportune moment. King Henry was becoming impatient with Katharine, because she had not provided him with a son. In a moment of irritation he was persuaded to sign a warrant for her arrest.

Doctor Wendy, the King's physician, who sympathised with the Protestants, came to warn Katharine and begged her to get rid of her books. She was much affeared and took to her bed. She wept loudly and cried that she was too young to die. Fortunately for her Henry's leg became worse and he sent for her. He needed a capable nurse with gentle hands and Katharine had found a new soothing ointment. His leg, it seemed, was her salvation.

The next day they sat in the rose garden. The King seemed to be in good spirits as they conversed amicably together. Lady Tyrwhit and I kept at a distance. Presently Sir Thomas Wriothesley appeared with an armed guard.

The King demanded to know what he meant by disturbing them. Sir Thomas replied that he had come to arrest the Queen, and escort her to the Tower. Katharine turned pale and all but swooned but spake not a word. The King rose from his seat and shouted to Sir Thomas to be gone or else it would be the worse for him. The guard turned and marched away, followed by Sir Thomas, who looked furiously angry.

The following day I heard Katharine beg the King not to be too hard on the Chancellor, for she said, 'He was doubtless mistaken as to your Majesty's orders.' I saw the King pat her hand. He replied that she knew not how little the Chancellor deserved grace at her hands. Albeit she did know. She knew full well that Thomas Wriothesley was her enemy.

God be praised. Those hazardous days are past and Katharine is now happy with the man she loves.

August 3 1547

It was such a warm day yesterday that I decided to take my books and study in the garden. I took Dulcia with me for company.

I had been concentrating on my Greek translation for an hour when I noticed the little dog was missing. At first I was not concerned. I called her several times but when she did not appear, I looked for her in the herb garden and on the terrace, but she was nowhere to be found.

Seeing that I was much troubled, Phoebe ordered the servants to search and promised a reward to anyone who found her. As the day wore on I began to fret for I have grown very fond of the little creature.

Imagine my relief when Phoebe appeared at dusk with Dulcia in her arms. The dog was damp and dirty but obviously pleased to see me.

One of the kitchen maids had discovered her in the kitchen, hiding underneath a table. Phoebe said she was smelly and gave her a bath.

I was so pleased to have her back that I broke one of my own rules and allowed her to sleep on my bed.

November 4 1547

Parliament met today. Edward is busy with affairs of state.

Phoebe says the number of beggars is growing. They come daily for food. Before the Dissolution of the Monasteries the monks used to feed them. Now they have nowhere to go, but roam the countryside begging for food.

December 22 1547

A happy ending to the year. Katharine told me she is expecting a child in August. I am so glad for her. She had given up hope of ever having a child of her own, for she has had three childless marriages and has now reached the age of thirty-six. She deserves this happiness. She has devoted her life to caring for others. Thomas is delighted. The child is to be born at Sudeley Castle. They have already chosen names, Thomas for a boy and Mary for a girl.

Phoebe says it is a serious matter to be having a first child at the age of thirty-six. I shall pray for Katharine's safe delivery.

January 16 1548

Sir Hugh Platt has been caught cheating at cards. He plays wearing a ring which has been set with a tiny mirror so that he can see his opponent's cards. Phoebe found this very droll and seemed surprised when I said he should be denounced as a cheat and a rogue.

February 13 1548

Christmas and Epiphany passed quietly this year. Edward complained of pains in his arms and legs. He sleeps badly. Doctor Cardano prescribed laudanum in small doses.

On Christmas Day we sat by the fire and listened to the King's musicians playing some new madrigals by one Thomas Tallys. Edward gave me some of his verses to read. We delight in each other's company. Since he became King we see little of each other as he spends much of the time at Greenwich. He told me he misses Katharine. She has been a mother to him. We both love her dearly.

I learned from Edward that his uncle, Thomas Seymour, sends him money secretly through his servant Fowler.

February 21 1548

Katharine, Elizabeth and I have been at Hampton Court for the past week. Thomas is away on one of his peregrinations.

Hampton Court is my favourite place. Edward was born there. It is full of memories. Sometimes when I walk in the cloisters I fancy I hear echoes of the past. I picture Anne Boleyn dancing merrily with King Henry and I imagine I hear young Catherine Howard calling Henry's name in desperation as she runs through the gallery towards the chapel. Alas, she called in vain. Ere she reached the chapel door the guards captured her, and her screams were drowned by the singing in the chapel.

It was on this very day six years ago that she was beheaded. Poor Catherine, so young and carefree. It is sad to die so young.

March 5 1548

When Phoebe brushed my hair last night I mentioned that I wished it was the colour of Elizabeth's. Her hair is red-gold and she has curls in abundance. My hair is straight and sand coloured. I have pale eyebrows and freckles and my eyes are grey. I am quite plain.

Phoebe says handsome is as handsome does, and in her opinion Elizabeth is over-bold for a young maiden. She said I should not sit in the sun or my freckles will multiply. Dear Phoebe. I live in constant fear that she will look to be wed and leave me. She has several admirers. Amos Swinford the head groom has asked for her hand, but she refused him, saying he was too fond of dicing and cards. Truly I do not think she wants to leave me.

April 15 1548

Phoebe gathers news as a bee gathers pollen, especially when it comes from the West Country. Apparently a certain Thomas Wynter was charged by the Council to remove all images remaining in any church or chapel in Cornwall. He arrived at Helston on April the fifth with one William Body. The people were roused and poured in from the surrounding parishes. When Body began to destroy the images in Helston church he was set upon and stabbed to death. The crowd then turned upon Thomas and served him in like manner. Needless to say all efforts to identify the culprits have failed.

April 19 1548

There has been flooding in Northampton as a result of a great storm, with much thunder and lightning. Hours of heavy rain cased the floods, which carried away bridges and drowned horses, men and cattle.

One bridge was swept away while a man was crossing it on horseback. The horse was drowned, but the man, by great good fortune, was carried to the river bank, and by clinging to the roots of a willow was able to haul himself out of the water.

April 21 1548

A ship anchored in the Thames reports that there is plague in Calais. A certain Captain De Hoogh died on board his ship together with fifty of his crew.

April 23 1548

When I returned from riding today I noticed that Bella was limping. I told Amos Swinford and he examined her feet. He found one of her shoes to be loose and he will take her to the farrier today.

As I was leaving, he enquired if Phoebe was well and sent his respectful regards. Later when I told Phoebe, she blushed and said he was over-familiar and presumptuous to send a message to the maid through the mistress.

I teased her and asked if she regretted having refused his proposal. Her reply was terse. 'He is not for me,' was all she would say. I fear Amos Swinford is hoping in vain.

May 30 1548

Katharine and I have come to Sudeley Castle. We came to prepare the nursery. Katharine wants to be certain that all is in readiness though the birth is still two months off.

The nursery is a pleasant room, hung with new tapestries depicting the twelve months of the year. Two chairs covered with gold cloth stand ready and a gilded cradle has been specially made.

Katharine is so happy. She can scarcely believe she is to be a mother at last. She has had a troublesome pregnancy, but she says it will all be worthwhile when she holds her child in her arms. I pray she will come through her ordeal safely and the child will be healthy.

The gardens here are lovely. After dinner Katharine and I strolled along the Yew Walk. The trees are at their best. Beyond the park there are delightful views of the Cotswold Hills. The air is fragrant with the scent of flowers and herbs. Butterflies are thick on the buddleia bushes and bees hum in the lavender.

It gives me pleasure to see Katharine so contented. She told me she has everything she ever dreamed of, a loving husband, a delightful home, and soon a child to make her happiness complete. It had been a perfect day.

June 21 1548

News reached us that Bishop Gardiner has been arrested and is in the Tower. He has been speaking against the marriage of priests and the freedom of the people to complain about the Mass.

Edward would have no choice but to imprison him. I cannot feel pity for the Bishop. I have not forgotten that he was involved with Chancellor Wriothesley in the plot to incriminate Katharine two years ago.

We often speak of the days at Chelsea when Katharine, Edward, Elizabeth and I would discuss religion and have friendly arguments. There was little disagreement for we are all Protestant.

July 4 1548

We had been at the Chelsea Dower House only two days when it happened. It is like a bad dream. Alas, if only it <u>were</u> a dream. I was with Katharine when she found them together. She opened the door and there they were in each other's arms, kissing passionately, mindless of our presence. When they became aware of us they sprang apart guiltily.

I shall never forget the look on Katharine's face as long as I live. The shock, the horror and finally the pain. Dear Katharine, who has never knowingly hurt anyone in her life. Elizabeth averted her eyes and brushed past us as she fled from the room. Thomas had the grace to look abashed. He tried to laugh it off, saying it meant nothing, it was but a game. Katharine did not hear him. She turned and walked away as if bemused, muttering, 'I have been blind.' I could find no words to comfort her.

July 5 1548

I have never seen Katharine like this. For hours she has been weeping and pacing up and down. Thomas tried to soothe her but she would not listen. She begged him to leave her and at last he went.

I can imagine her thoughts. This was a marriage that was to have brought her true happiness. Now, in one brief moment, that happiness has been destroyed.

She sobbed. She cried that she has been betrayed. I begged her to be calm for the sake of the child. I began to fear for her reason. Finally, worn out with weeping, she allowed me to help her to bed. I doubt she will sleep tonight. I know I shall not. My heart is filled with pity for her, and I can think of nothing that will comfort her. I find it hard to forgive Elizabeth for Katharine was like a mother to her.

Woe follows upon woe. News has just come that William Grindal has died. We all liked him. He was a good and patient tutor and showed me much kindness.

July 7 1548

Katharine seems calmer today. This morning she sent for Elizabeth and told her she must leave at once. She is to go to Sir Anthony Denny's house at Cheshunt. Kat Ashley is indignant. She blames Thomas, for, she says, Elizabeth is but fifteen years old.

I went to Katharine's chamber. I did not know what to say to her. I could only embrace her in silent sympathy. She wept quietly and I wept with her. She told me she has decided to go back to Sudeley Castle and stay there until the child is born. She wants me to accompany her. She calls me her little comforter. How I wish I knew how to comfort her now.

August 3 1548

The move to Sudeley Castle went smoothly. Besides Katharine and myself there were two maids of honour, three women of the bedchamber and one hundred and twenty gentlemen and yeomen.

Katharine's chaplain, Miles Coverdale, is expected tomorrow. This morning I sat with Katharine and read to her. I showed her my collection of Latin proverbs. Collecting these has become a hobby of mine.

Later we inspected the nursery. Everything is in readiness for the coming child. Thomas is away at the present time, but he has said he will be here for the birth. Katharine does not seem to care whether he is here or not. She does not speak of him. She has not recovered from the shock of finding Elizabeth in his arms. I fear his presence can only cause her distress.

August 5 1548

News from Scotland. Mary Stuart has sailed for France. A marriage has been arranged between Mary and the Dauphin Francis. She never knew her father, who died when she was one week old. She is not yet six years old and over-young to be parted from her mother to live in a strange land. I pity her.

August 10 1548

Katharine is very listless. When I said I thought she looked tired she complained that the peacocks woke her too early with their raucous cries.

We sat in the rose garden near the sundial. The sun was warm. The bees hummed around us and the doves were cooing softly. Sudeley is very lovely at this time of the year. From where we were sitting we could look across the Cotswold hills. I wondered where Thomas was. He should be here at this time, though his presence will give Katharine little comfort.

She said she would like to go into the little chapel of St Mary and offer up a prayer. She could not kneel, being so near her time, but she closed her eyes and prayed. I too, most fervently, for her safe delivery and future happiness.

August 29 1548

Katharine's pains began this morning. They have sent a messenger for Thomas. His absences from Sudeley have been more and more protracted. Since that fateful day at Chelsea Katharine has treated him like a stranger. She has never forgiven him for destroying her happiness. This should have been a time of rejoicing for them.

Lady Tyrwhit has been with Katharine all day. I went to the chamber at noon, but I saw at once that there was little I could do. Katharine was in agony and did not seem to know where she was. Seeing my distress Lady Tyrwhit thought it best I should leave.

I went to the chapel. I sat there for a long time in that peaceful place. I stared up at the high panelled oak roof with the bosses designed as Tudor roses. The sun shone through the stained glass window above the altar, depicting Christ on the cross and threw into shadow the marble reredos beneath. If all went well the child would be baptised at the marble font. I prayed earnestly that all would go well. I have grown to love Katharine, with her gentle ways and her loving heart. She has been like a mother to me.

As I sat there in the peace of that quiet place there came upon me a heaviness of spirit and a foreboding of sorrow. I rose and went out into the garden. The sky was overcast and black storm clouds loured sullenly over the Cotswold Hills.

August 30 1548

Katharine was safely delivered of a daughter early today. The child is healthy and is to be christened Mary. I am to be her godmother.

We are all anxious for Katharine. She has a fever and is wandering in her mind. Lady Tyrwhit came to tell me of the birth. She looked very tired. I made her rest awhile and brought her a glass of wine. She told me that Thomas had arrived just after the birth. He tried to take Katharine in his arms, but she would have none of it, and turned away from him muttering incoherently.

They brought the child to her. She stared at it but refused to hold it. She seized Lady Tyrwhit's hand and whispered, 'I am not well served. They use me ill that have done them no wrong.' Lady Tyrwhit sat with her until she fell asleep.

September 2 1548

I was with Katharine throughout the morning. I held her hand and spoke quietly to her but she did not open her eyes. She lay there quite peacefully, and mercifully was in no pain.

Lady Tyrwhit looked at me and shook her head. The attendants did not speak but I read in their faces that they offered no hope. I cannot bear to think of it.

Dear sweet Katharine, who never did a mean thing or spoke an unkind word. At a time like this I cannot see God's purpose. Truly it is hard to say, 'Thy will be done.'

September 7 1548

Early this morning while it was yet dark Phoebe awakened me. She did not need to speak. I saw in her tear-stained face that Katharine was dead.

I have wept until I have no more tears left. I shall never see her again, that kind and loving lady. I shall never walk with her among the fragrant herbs and flowers on a summer evening.

One joyous year of love was all the happiness she knew after three loveless marriages. Then came disillusionment and despair.

Thomas is closeted in his chamber and will see no one. I am loth to judge him. Yet I believe Katharine felt that because of his infidelity life was no longer worth living. Even the coming child could not compensate for his betrayal. In one brief moment she had fallen from the heights of happiness to the depths of despair. Afterwards she had no wish to live, for Thomas was her world.

September 9 1548

We have just returned from Katharine's funeral. Thomas was not present at the ceremony as is customary. The walls of the chapel were hung with black. Miles Coverdale preached the sermon. I scarcely heard his words. My thoughts were all of Katharine, her kindness, her sweet nature and her faithful heart. How hurt she had been by Thomas's behaviour. She had never recovered from the shock of finding them together. She was too trusting, too vulnerable. Such people are always hurt the most.

I wept for myself and my great loss. I did not weep for Katharine, for she is at peace. No one can ever hurt her again. I shall miss her more than any words can tell. As for Thomas, he must live with his conscience and the knowledge that he was the one who destroyed her happiness. I cannot pity him. Because of him I have lost a dear friend and the babe a mother.

September 12 1548

I went to Katharine's room early this morning. I sought a small keepsake for her remembrance. I found her prayer book with the red velvet cover, which King Henry had given her. I will treasure it always and it shall be a reminder of her.

As I picked it up a piece of paper fluttered to the floor. It was a verse written in Katharine's hand. As I read it I wept unashamedly.

> Come not when I am in my coffin laid,
> Weep not to see me lowered into clay,
> Sigh not to see my eyelids closed in death,
> Remember that you broke my heart today.

It was signed and dated July 6th, the day after she discovered the truth.

September 14 1548

The babe thrives in the care of a wet nurse. She is a pretty child. She was christened in the chapel today. Katharine herself had chosen the name Mary. I wonder how the child will fare in this world, without a mother. Arrangements are being made for her to live with an uncle when she is five years old.

My heart is heavy. I am to return to Bradgate tomorrow.

October 6 1548

Edward has sent me a birthday gift, a set of twelve buttons enamelled with purple and yellow pansies. Elizabeth sent me a black velvet purse to keep combs in. The buttons are very pretty. Edward enclosed a loving letter with them. He says he misses Katharine. She was the nearest thing to a mother he has ever known.

His cough troubles him a great deal. His doctor has prescribed honey, which he hopes will ease it, and comfrey which is good for weakness of the chest.

He wrote of the happy days when we studied together. He is making good progress with his Greek and Latin under the supervision of Doctor Richard Cox.

He has summoned his sister Mary to court, but she excused herself saying she was not well enough to travel. She knows she would not be able to attend Mass if she were at court. She leans towards Spain, for it was her mother's country and the Emperor is her great-uncle. She is a fervent Catholic and has always disapproved of Edward's Protestant upbringing. She never discusses religion with him for she knows of his love of the Reformed Faith.

November 7 1548

Pheobe came with disturbing news. Kat Ashley and Thomas Parry, Elizabeth's servants, have been taken for questioning. The Council are attempting to implicate Thomas, Lord Sudeley, by uncovering a liaison between him and Elizabeth. Wild rumours abound. People are saying he poisoned Katharine in order to be free to court Elizabeth. The rumour is said to have been started by his sister-in-law the Duchess of Somerset who has always hated him.

Elizabeth must be fearful. Kat Ashley is devoted to her, but a prisoner under questioning can be made to say anything.

Lord Sudeley was warned publicly by Lord Russell that if he had ambitions to marry Elizabeth he would be courting disaster, but he merely laughed. I wonder if Lord Russell is aware that he proposed to Elizabeth last year.

January 17 1549

Thomas Seymour, Lord Sudeley, has been arrested and taken to the Tower. His recklessness is beyond belief. It seems he has been conspiring with pirates in the Bristol Channel to share their spoils. It was also discovered that he has built up a store of ammunition and boasts that he has ten thousand men who can be called to arms at any time.

When summoned by his brother the Duke of Somerset he ignored the order and was immediately arrested.

February 2 1549

We always eat fish on Fridays, so the new Act will not greatly affect our household. The Act orders people to abstain from eating meat on Fridays and Saturdays. This is to encourage the fishing industry and increase the size of the fishing fleet.

Thomas Cranmer has produced an English Book of Common Prayer. The Act of Uniformity will compel churches to use this book from November onwards and the Mass may no longer be said in Latin.

February 4 1549

My thoughts have been with Elizabeth. Sir Robert Tyrwhit questioned her for hours but she would admit nothing that might endanger Thomas Seymour. She loves him, of that I am certain. What must she be thinking at this moment, knowing he is in danger yet forced to hide her feelings? She must be nigh frantic with worry and with good cause. For Thomas Seymour is in peril of his life. There are thirty-three charges of treason against him.

February 14 1549

Thomas Seymour has been charged with unlawfully seeking the hand of the King's sister Elizabeth in marriage. He has been found guilty and a Bill of Attainder has been issued against him.

He is to be executed on the twentieth day of March. When Sir Robert Tyrwhit told Elizabeth the verdict she kept her emotions in check and said nothing.

March 21 1549

Yesterday Thomas Seymour went to the block. He was beheaded without being given a chance to speak in his own defence. This was by command of his brother Edward. The people murmured. They will not forget this. I am glad Katharine was not here to see this day. Yet she might have saved him from this fate, for had she lived he could not have been accused of seeking marriage with Elizabeth. She never stopped loving him in spite of everything. Few women could resist his charm.

I wondered what Edward was thinking as he signed the death warrant. Thomas had been his favourite uncle. Edward Seymour must have poisoned the King's mind against his brother. They say he died bravely. Among the onlookers on Tower Hill were women who wept when the handsome head was held up by the executioner.

When Elizabeth was told it was all over she appeared to be quite unmoved. She said calmly, 'This day died a man of much wit and very little judgement.' Bishop Latimer was less restrained. He said, 'He was a wicked man and the realm is well rid of him. He was covetous, ambitious and seditious.'

Following the execution Edward would not allow Elizabeth to come to court. He said that a meeting between them was not desirable at this time. I wondered if he feared her reproaches, or whether he was angry that she should have caused gossip about herself and Thomas. For her part, she was too ill and too tired to care. Thomas's death had left her desolate.

April 14 1549

I took a basket into the garden that I might cut some of the best roses. My sister Catherine found me there. It has been such a beautiful spring day. We walked in the knot garden and fed the doves. Catherine had hoped to see father but he is seldom at home these days. He spends much time with the Earl of Northumberland.

My tutor John Aylmer tells me that he has obtained a copy of Tyndale's translation of the New Testament. I would like to read it but I should have to do so in secret because it is forbidden.

May 17 1549

I miss Katharine so much. Sometimes I can scarcely believe that she and Thomas are both gone. She and I spent many happy hours discussing books and religion. I know that Erasmus has written a book called *The Praise of Folly*. I would like to read it.

June 9 1549

Today is Whitsun Day. The Act of Uniformity comes into effect today authorising Cranmer's New English Prayer Book which now comes into use for the first time. Opinions are much divided. Some people are pleased to read it in English. Others still prefer the Latin version.

July 2 1549

There has been trouble with the peasants over the Enclosure Act and common land. Some lords have enclosed their demesnes and meadows so that peasants may no longer pasture their cattle. There has been some lawlessness in rural areas. In Norfolk twenty thousand peasants tried to seize Yarmouth, demanding the end of the Enclosure Act. The Duke of Warwick was sent with German mercenaries and three thousand of the peasants fell in battle. Their leader Robert Kett died on the gallows with three hundred other rebels.

I asked John Aylmer why there was so much unrest. He says the churches are empty, people neglect their religion and there is a fearful ignorance. Children of sixteen do not know the Lord's Prayer. Some priests are unable to repeat the Ten Commandments, which is a shameful state of affairs.

July 3 1549

It seems there was a great murder done on Saturday last in a tavern in Shoe Lane.

One Captain Lovett was shot by one Symons. They were playing cards and in drink.

Captain Lovett, who was killed, is a kinsman of Lord Crewe. What will come of it?

July 4 1549

Robert Ascham found me in the rose garden. He had called to bid us farewell for he is to leave for Italy next week. He asked me why I had not joined the hunt. I told him of my revulsion at the killing of any animal and of my love of study. He was surprised to find me reading Platos' *Phaedo* in Greek. He made me promise to write to him in Greek while he is away. He told me Edward has made much progress in Greek and he translates quite easily the Latin of Cicero's philosophy into Greek.

He agrees with John Aylmer that learning is more important than experience. He declared that it is possible to learn more in one year from books than from twenty year's experience. It is not only safer, it is infinitely less costly.

A sea – captain, he said, who learned his craft by many shipwrecks, must be a very unhappy man.

I confess I envied him his Sojourn in Italy and I wished him a safe and pleasant voyage.

July 5 1549

Word has come of a rebellion in the West Country against the new prayer book. People always mislike change. The rebels are demanding the restoration of the Mass. It is said ten thousand people marched from Devon and Cornwall. The people are demanding the Latin service in Cornwall because they do not speak English. In the city of Exeter the authorities obeyed the King and defended the city, which the rebels have besieged. They demand that the Mass should be said in Latin, as heretofore. Most churchmen have obeyed the law, but the common people seem ready to risk their lives to preserve the religion to which they are accustomed.

August 6 1549

Royal troops led by Lord Russell, Earl of Bedford, have entered the city of Exeter. The rising is ended. Robert Welsh, the vicar of St Thomas, a parish just outside the city, was seized as a traitor and hanged from his own church tower in full vestments. It was said afterwards that but for his intervention the rebels would have set fire to the city by shooting flaming arrows. John Aylmer said the Western Rebellion had to be nipped in the bud. If these rebels had reached London and joined with others of the same persuasion it could have resulted in civil war.

Pheobe is affronted. She has learned from her uncle, Robert Yeandall, that cannon from Topsham were used by the rebels besieging the city of Exeter.

August 10 1549

The Council has tried in vain to force Mary to abandon the Mass. She will not agree. They told her there would be no exceptions. The Act of Uniformity must be obeyed by all. Albeit the Emperor is her cousin and they do not wish to rouse his anger. After some consideration they told her she may hear Mass privately in her own apartments.

John Dudley, Earl of Warwick, has taken the title Duke of Northumberland.

August 18 1549

I have been reading the new prayer book. One sentence
in particular seems to be me to express what I feel.
'Christ's Gospel is not a ceremonial law. It is a religion
to serve God, not in the bondage of ritual but in the
freedom of the spirit.' I have always tried to worship
God in the true way, divested of superstition.

September 5 1549

Dear Katharine died one year ago today. Lady Tyrwhit wrote that the child Mary is thriving. Sometimes Katharine seems very near. I hold her prayer book in my hand and I can almost feel her presence. It is as if her spirit hovers near me and she is ever in my thoughts.

October 5 1549

Tomorrow will be my twelfth anniversary. I have had my portrait painted by Master John. He sketched me at first, then he painted my head and shoulders. When the portrait was half completed the dress was draped on a wooden dolly and he painted the details from that. This was father's idea. It ensured that I did not spend too many hours away from my study. It is the most elaborate dress I have ever owned, made of cloth of silver lined with fur. It has a crimson and gold underskirt with brilliant jewels. I wore a jewelled coif and six rings.

October 11 1549

Last night I had a strange dream. I dreamed that I stood on the edge of a deep dark chasm. I tried to move away from the edge but I could not move. I raised my eyes and saw Katharine standing on the opposite side. She was dressed all in white and she looked more beautiful than I had ever seen her. I called her name and begged her to help me, but she spoke not a word. She beckoned me to come to her yet I could not because of the chasm between us. As I stood there the earth beneath my feet crumbled and I was hurled into space. I screamed in terror and awoke with the echo of the scream in my ears and my heart pounding. The moon was shining full on my face and the dark corners of the room were full of ghostly shadows.

Albeit it was but a dream. Yet I could sleep no more but lay awake until dawn came, my thoughts full of Katharine.

December 15 1549

Elizabeth is back in favour. She is to be at court for Christmas. Mary was invited also but she refused to come pleading illness. She knows that Edward will expect her to attend the Protestant services. She is stubborn. She will never forego the mass.

Queen Katherine would have been proud of her daughter. Mary would like to bring back the Mass and the old allegiance to the Pope. Pray Heaven she will never have the opportunity.

January 10 1550

We heard today that a new pope has been declared. He is Julius the third. Mary gives regular audiences to the Spanish ambassador. Her dearest wish is to bring England back to Rome. While Edward lives the Protestant religion is secure. God grant him a long life.

The royal chaplains are now reading the services entirely in English. They preach justification by faith alone, which means an individual religion.

February 3 1550

Today I received a letter from Edward. It was brief. He has much to attend to. He tells me he still finds time for study under the guidance of his tutor, John Cheke. I would that I could study with him.

It pains me to read that his cough is still troublesome and his headaches more frequent. Poor Edward, plagued with ill-health yet ever patient. I wish we could be together as in the old days. Since he became King everything has changed.

March 14 1550

It has rained all day without ceasing, and the sky is dark. I had hoped to ride today for Bella needs the exercise. I spent the morning reading Sir Thomas More's *Dialogue of Comfort* which he wrote while he was a prisoner in the Tower. Dear Katharine gave me this book shortly before she died. This afternoon I translated a passage of Scripture.

Dulcia is so good. She sits at my feet while I study. If I speak to her she wags her tail vigorously. Phoebe, who says that all dogs are bothersome, has reluctantly admitted that Dulcia is well-behaved. Phoebe has found a cure for freckles in Doctor William Turner's *Herbal and Dictionary of Plants'* She says they can be cured by washing the face with elder leaves distilled in May and then splashing the skin with lemon water. When summer comes I will put this cure to the test.

April 13 1550

It is now several months since Cranmer's prayer book was approved by Parliament. All services in Latin have been abolished. We hear of wholesale destruction of images in the churches. I can imagine Mary's anger and frustration as the country moves further and further away from Rome.

April 22 1550

Spring is here. The fields are full of daisies. Along the banks of the river the yellow marsh marigolds glow in abundance. Primroses and wild violets bloom along the hedgerows.

I sent some of my verses to Edward. We often wrote verses together when we were in the schoolroom. I doubt he has time to write poetry these days. He is much occupied with his Council and state duties.

This morning I sat in the herb garden. I did not neglect my studies for I took with me the new book by William Thomas. It is called *Principle Rules of the Italian Grammer*. Phoebe says I study overmuch. She refuses to believe me when I say that I find study to be both a pleasure and a satisfaction.

June 10 1550

Pheobe has been to see Amos Swinford and brings disquieting news about Edward. He was riding in the park this morning with several attendants. When they returned to the stables Amos stepped forward to hold Edward's horse. Instead of dismounting, Edward suddenly fell forward with his head on the horse's neck. He was carried at once to his bed and attended by Doctor Cardano, who says that he is suffering from exhaustion and must rest.

I will say a prayer for him.

August 3 1550

My father sent a messenger to say that he wished to have speech with me. I hastened to the library, wondering what I had done to incur his displeasure. I was relieved to find him in good humour and in earnest conversation with a visitor.

It was one Henry Roper, a distant relative of William Roper, who married Sir Thomas More's daughter, Margaret. I soon realised why I had been summoned. Henry Roper is a scholar. We conversed in both Latin and Greek. He complimented me afterwards and told my father he should be proud of me.

My father never praises me, but I am sometimes called to meet his friends and converse with them about books I have read.

October 14 1550

Elizabeth went to visit Edward on his birthday, two days ago. She is concerned for his health. She carried a letter from me and he was pleased to receive it. He did not feel well enough to reply immediately but he sent his love and a bookmark embroidered with a sprig of rosemary.

He has been unable to ride from Whitehall to Westminster, and is suffering from painful headaches. Rest in a darkened room sometimes brings relief. I would I could help him, but all I can do is assure him of my love and remember him in my prayers.

November 7 1550

Edward is confined to his bed again. The doctors have bled him but to no avail. His health becomes steadily worse. He was never strong. He suffers much yet he seldom complains. I would we were all in the schoolroom together as we used to be, for he was happy then. I will write him a letter. He must not think that I have forgotten him. Dear Edward, so valiant a spirit in so frail a body.

December 10 1550

A cold north-east wind is blowing today. I pity the poor beggars. They once sought alms, food and shelter from the monasteries. Now they have nowhere to go. Yet I believe Cromwell was right to expose the evil practices that went on in the convents and monasteries. There was a sad lack of discipline.

Many priests were using women as their wives. Abbots who were deposed for serious immorality found themselves comfortably pensioned. Tales abounded of clandestine marriages between monks and nuns, of drunkedness, dice, cards and unlawful games. One convent was conveniently situated near a lime pit where, it was said, the nuns threw their unwanted illegitimate babies.

All these things had brought the monasteries into disrepute and drastic measures were necessary. The evil had to be rooted out.

January 8 1551

There was a very hard frost last night. Amos Swinford told Phoebe that the coach from Bath arrived very late and the coachman refused to alight. When he was seized it was discovered that the poor man had frozen to death on his seat, the whip still in his hand. The horses, having traversed the same roads countless times, had continued the journey without guidance, none of the passengers being any the wiser.

January 10 1551

A sumptuous banquet was held at Greenwich at Epiphany. Elizabeth sat in the place of honour below Edward. Mary was not present. She still refuses to give up the Mass. The Protestants fear her. They are asking themselves what will happen when she comes to the throne. They note Edward's state of health and it gives them cause to fear for the future.

March 5 1551

There has been much talk of a marriage between Edward and nine year old Mary Stuart, who is still in France. It is but hearsay. Mary is already promised to the Dauphin Francis, and has been living at the French court for the last three years.

June 4 1551

When tidings from Devonshire reach us they are already one week old, so when Phoebe received the sad news, it was already too late for her to attend the funeral of her cousin.

Lucy Elyot was drowned off Exmouth together with the boatman. It seems a sudden squall overturned the boat. Lucy was twenty-three years old. She and Phoebe had grown up together. Phoebe is quite inconsolable. The sea has robbed her of a father and now a cousin.

July 10 1551

Mary has been ill and is said to be suffering from melancholy.

Word has come that the sweating sickness is at Shrewsbury this summer. There have been reports that nine hundred people have died in a fortnight. A man may be merry at dinner and dead at supper, so swift is the progress of the disease.

July 12 1551

Edward has gone to Hampton Court because the sweating sickness is spreading. He will be safer there and the country air will be good for him. He can enjoy the beautiful gardens and the river running close by. I would I were with him. Hampton Court is such a delightful place in summer, bordered by the Thames, in a lovely setting surrounded by rose gardens and fountains. Edward and I were always happy there. If his father had not died we might be happy still. I miss him.

August 2 1551

Doctor Cardano came to see us with the latest news of the plague. He told us that in Drury Lane he did see two or three houses marked with a red cross upon the door and 'Lord have mercy on us' written there. In the street he did overtake two women crying and carrying a man's coffin between them. He supposed it was the husband of one of them.

August 14 1551

Miles Coverdale has completed his translation of the Bible into English, an awesome task. He has been appointed Bishop of Exeter. He is a Yorkshireman and an alumnus of Cambridge University. He is to be consecrated on August 30th at Croydon by Archbishop Cranmer. He favours the New Religion and has many Protestant friends in Switzerland, Germany and Holland.

When he was at Sudeley Castle he and Katharine had long discussions about the New Religion. It was while I was with them at Sudeley that we heard of the sad death of William Grindal at Cambridge. He had been our tutor and was a particular favourite of Elizabeth's.

October 6 1551

Today is my fourteenth anniversary. It is a lovely autumn day. I took More's *Dialogue of Comfort* and found a quiet corner in the knot garden. My thoughts turned, as they often do, to Katharine. I miss her loving companionship and her gentle ways.

I have received some delightful gifts, including an alabaster comfort box and a silver cabinet of exquisite workmanship to hold notepaper. My favourite gift was Edward's. It was a copy of Erasmus's book *The Praise of Folly* which I have long wanted to read.

December 15 1551

Edward Seymour has written to Elizabeth from the Tower. He begged her to speak to Edward on his behalf. She replied that it would be unwise to become involved at this time.

She told me with some bitterness that she could not forget his indifference when his brother Thomas went to the block. Although nearly three years have passed since Thomas was beheaded, I believe Elizabeth still thinks of him often, and of the excitement he brought into her life. I have no doubt that she loved him, but she was wise enough to see that nothing could come of it.

January 16 1552

Parliament met today, the first time for two years.

Edward's health continues to cause us all concern. The people are wondering what will happen if he should die. Mary would succeed. She would endeavour to bring Catholicism back to the country. The people are not sure that they want an ardent Catholic to rule them. Mary is almost fanatical in her religious beliefs. This is due to her mother, Katherine of Aragon, who brought Mary up close to both Catholic and Spanish influences and instilled in her an unshakeable faith in Rome.

January 23 1552

The Duke of Somerset was beheaded on Tower Hill yesterday, three years after his brother Thomas met the same fate. He was found guilty of plotting to secure the throne for his heirs. People said he had become Protector merely because he was the King's uncle. He died bravely, protesting his innocence.

John Dudley, having assumed the title 'Duke of Northumberland and Protector,' has consolidated his position and has great influence over Edward. At his instigation a Privy Council has been set up to examine the King's financial problems.

February 4 1552

The Castle and Manor of Sudeley have been granted to Katharine's brother, William Parr, Marquess of Northampton. Little has been heard of his three year old niece Mary Seymour. She is believed to be living with Lady Suffolk in Oxfordshire. William Parr, as her guardian, has control of her considerable fortune.

March 1 1552

Edward has measles. Naturally the doctors are worried.
He is not strong. Fortunately it seems to be only a slight
case and they expect him to recover with careful nursing.
My thoughts and my prayers are with him, as always.

April 15 1552

I write today with great sadness. Dear little Dulcia is dead. I was in the garden with her this morning. I turned to call her and found her lying on her side. She appeared to be having some sort of fit. I spoke to her soothingly. She tried to rise but fell back and then was still. I shall miss her so much. She has been my little companion and was devoted to me. She shall be buried in the shrubbery and Amos shall make her a small headstone. I have told him to inscribe on it the words 'Dulcia 1549 -1552. *Semper fidelis.*'

June 17 1552

My parents punish me for the least thing. It seems I can do nothing right. If I speak what is in my mind it is wrong. If I remain silent it is wrong. It is so hard to please them. I know my father is irritated because I prefer to study when he would like me to join the hunt. It is bootless to try to explain.

August 18 1552

Amos Swinford told Phoebe he was on Tower Hill this morning when he heard a tremendous bang. People ran from the Tower shouting that there had been an explosion. It transpired that someone had allowed a spark to fall on a mortar containing gunpowder. Seven men were burned and eight were maimed.

October 30 1552

I have been on a visit to Newhall at Mary's invitation. She is worried about Edward. She talked about him a great deal and spoke of the happy times they had spent together. She told me Edward loved me 'as a sister' and said she knew that I was very fond of him. She has been receiving very disquieting reports about his health. I was not able to reassure her, for I know that Edward is very ill.

December 10 1552

Doctor Cardano has been visiting Edward who has a rasping cough. He is spitting blood, and has become very thin. The doctor described him as 'an angel in human form.' Dear Edward, he is so patient in his suffering.

December 31 1552

We all gathered at Greenwich for Christmas. Edward attempted to join in the festivities and make merry, but he coughed persistently and looked very pale. He was content to sit and talk with me. We spoke of the old days before he became King and how happy we were in the schoolroom. By mutual consent neither of us mentioned Thomas Seymour. I often wonder how Edward felt about signing his death warrant. He had been so fond of his uncle. Of course there had been the curious incident when Thomas had shot Edward's pet dog. Edward would find it hard to forgive that. He must have been influenced by the Council. They made out a good case against Thomas.

January 6 1553

Edward discussed with me ways of helping the poor and needy. He has given the Palace of Bridewell as a workhouse for poor people and arranged that St Thomas's Hospital should be used for the treatment of the infirm and ill. Christ's Hospital has been turned into a school for poor scholars.

It gives us both great satisfaction if we can think of ways to help the poor, of which alas there are many.

February 13 1553

Last night a great wind did blow. Old Samuel, the coachman, who is nigh on seventy years old, says he cannot remember such a tempest in his lifetime. In the garden five great trees grouped together were all blown down. Hundreds of oaks and beeches were blown down in the forest near Epping. It was dangerous to be out of doors, tiles being flung from the rooftops.

Lady Gerard, who lives in Covent Garden, was killed by the fall of her house while she was still in her bed. Boats tied up on the Thames were ripped from their moorings and blown away. Just before dawn the storm abated to the relief of all.

March 3 1553

Parliament met today. Edward was present but it was plain to all that he is far from well.

I have learned from my sister Catherine that my father has arranged a match for her. She is to marry Lord Herbert, son of the Earl of Pembroke. She says she does not love him, but he is kind and considerate and she believes he will make a good husband.

Phoebe says love often comes after marriage, but I could never marry where I did not love.

March 23 1553

Yesterday was Catherine's wedding day. She is now Lady Herbert. She looked very pale but beautiful in a gown of ivory embroidered with pearls. My father was in a good humour. He and the Earl of Pembroke talked and laughed together at the marriage feast.

When the bride and groom left for their honeymoon I slipped away. I went to sit in the garden but it was cold and a keen wind was blowing. I did not tarry long. Happy is the bride the sun shines on, they say, but the sun died not shine at all today.

April 3 1553

Phoebe tells me that nigh on eight hundred Protestants have emigrated to France and the Rhineland, among them friends of her Devonshire uncle. They anticipate the death of Edward and the succession of Mary. They fear persecution under a Catholic Queen and speak with dread of the Inquisition. Mary's ambition was always to restore England to Roman Catholicism and they say she may marry Philip of Spain to this end. At the same time many people think she will marry Edward Courtenay. They would prefer him to a foreigner.

I have heard gruesome tales about the Inquisition. The Spaniards would like to set it up in every country. It is important that England remains Protestant. Pray God that Edward lives for many years yet.

May 14 1553

Edward is gravely ill. The doctors are with him night and day. They say his illness is consumption. He coughs continuously and has a fever. I asked if I might go to him but he is too ill to see anyone. I will pray for him. It is all I can do. God send us good news of him.

May 15 1554

This morning I was summoned to the library. I found my father there with the Duke of Northumberland. He bade me sit down. Then he told me that a marriage had been arranged for me. I am to marry Guildford Dudley, fourth son of the Duke.

I was quite unprepared. I stammered that I would consider it. This reply made my father very angry. He said it is all arranged. I have never defied my father before but I was desperate. I blurted out that I did not wish to marry. My father ordered me to go to my room and stay there. I have been locked in all day. My mother came to me. She scolded me and said I was an undutiful daughter and doubtless a sound beating will help me to change my mind. I am so unhappy. Phoebe is forbidden to come to me.

What can I do? I have never loved anyone but Edward. If I could but see him I would plead with him to prevent this marriage. Yet I believe he fears Northumberland and is manipulated by him. My head aches. I have tried all day to think of a way out of this plight. There is no way out.

May 19 1553

I have been locked in my room for four days. They beat me on the first day but I would not yield. Each evening they have sent me a jug of water and a manchet of bread. This morning they sent the chaplain. He quoted the Fifth Commandment and spoke of duty and obedience.

I have always honoured my father and mother. I have never disobeyed them until now. I am weary from lack of sleep and I have wept until my eyes are red.

I can hold out no longer. I shall tell them that I will marry Guildford Dudley, but I am sick at heart.

May 22 1553

Guildford and I were married yesterday. The ceremony was held at the Duke's London house. It was a sombre occasion. The thoughts of all present were with the King who is known to be gravely ill.

I sat through the feasting and dancing as one in a dream. At last came the bedding ceremony. The candles were extinguished and we were alone in the darkness. Guildford broke the silence. He said he knew that I did not love him. He too had no wish to be married. He had been forced into the marriage by his father. It was his opinion that there was a conspiracy afoot. I asked him to tell me all he knew.

It transpired that one day early in May Guildford had been in the library. He had fallen asleep on a settle in front of the fire. He was awakened by loud voices which he recognised. They were the voices of his father and his brother Robert. His father shouted that Robert had been a fool, and if he had not rushed into marriage with an obscure country girl he might have been King of England. I was puzzled by this. I could only assume that the Duke had wished Robert to marry the Princess Mary, who was heir to the throne. Yet I am certain that when Mary chooses a husband he will be a Catholic. The Dudleys have always been firm Protestants. Risking his father's displeasure Robert married pretty little Amy Robsart. I feel sorry for her. He never brings her to court, but leaves her at home in his manor of Hemsley.

Guildford and I talked far into the night. I wondered why our marriage was so important to the Duke. I wished I knew what was in his mind. I lay there trying to make sense of it all. In the darkness Guildford reached across and took my hand in his. I think we both needed to be comforted. I feel that I am being swept away on a fast-flowing river and I do not know where it will carry me.

July 5 1553

Early today a terrible storm blew up. The thunder and lightening were awesome. It was the worst storm I have ever known. The doctors have given Edward but a few hours to live. They say he is very weak, and it is pitiful to see him trying to cough. It seems everything that can be done for him has been done.

I cannot imagine life without him.

For as long as I can remember he has been my dear friend and companion.

Life will be empty without him.

July 6 1553

How can I find the words to express my sorrow. Dear Edward died at nine o'clock this evening of consumption of the lungs. I was not able to see him.

I wanted to tell him that I shall always love him and that my marriage was not of my choosing. I believe he knew it. Mayhap he was too ill to care.

I shall never see him again. It is like losing a dear brother, yet he was more to me than a brother. He will always have a special place in my heart.

Now all his troubles are over. He is free from pain, for which I thank God, for they say he suffered greatly. His last words were, 'Lord God free me from this calamitous life.'

July 7 1553

I was at Syon House when my father came to me with the incredible news. He told me that Edward has named me successor in his last will. I stood there unable to speak. I could not believe what I was hearing. I know this is wrong. Everyone expects Mary to be Queen. Her father, Henry the Eighth, had decreed it in his will, first Edward, then Mary, then Elizabeth and fourthly myself. I could see the hand of Northumberland in this. He knew that Edward was dying when he arranged my marriage. He must have persuaded Edward to disregard his father's wishes and change the succession. My head was spinning. I tried to tell my father that I could not do this thing, but suddenly the room tilted and I fell to the floor in a swoon.

When I recovered it was plain that my father was far from pleased. He had expected me to welcome the news. He said it was my duty to save England from Catholicism. It was the will of God. He pointed out that Mary's goal had always been England's reunion with Rome. He said that Protestants would be persecuted. The Inquisition with all its terrors would come to our shores if Mary reigned.

I wondered how she felt, being cheated of the throne by her brother. She and I had always been friends. Now she would hate me and who could blame her. I hoped she would understand that this was none of my doing.

I listened to my father in silence. At last I knew the reason for my marriage. Northumberland wished to rule England through his son, Guildford. We should be as puppets manipulated by him to further his ambitions. I remembered the scene in the library which Guildford had recounted to me on our wedding night. It all made sense now.

My head aches. All I can think of is Edward's death. A light has gone out of my life. My father knows how I grieve for him. He used my grief to serve his purpose. He reminded me that this was Edward's last wish.

July 8 1553

I sailed down the river to the Tower today as the new reigning Sovereign. Surely it is all a dream. I told myself that I would soon awaken and find myself in my study with my books and my music.

I wore a brocade gown, richly embroidered, with long sleeves and a green and white bodice trimmed with gold thread. On my head I wore a white coif decorated with gems.

I was trembling as we entered the Tower. I walked under a canopy held by six noblemen. My mother held my train. Guildford walked beside me, richly attired. There was constraint between us. He has told me that his father advised him to insist on being called King. This I cannot agree to and I shall stand firm.

We were welcomed by the Lord Chancellor, the Marquis of Winchester and Sir John Brydges, the Lieutenant of the Tower. I entered the Royal Apartments to the sound of artillery.

Only Phoebe knows my true feelings. I have told her how unhappy I am. I have no wish to be Queen. I can imagine Mary's anger. How she must resent me. She has left Kenninghall and gone north in haste. She has reached Framlingham which belongs to the Catholic Duke of Norfolk.

The Catholics in the north will support her. Elizabeth is at Hatfield and conveniently indisposed. My father has had me proclaimed Queen. Nicholas Ridley has preached publicly at St Paul's Cross in support of me. He threatened Popery and tyranny should Mary enforce her claim. He declared that both she and Elizabeth are illegitimate.

My father-in-law the Duke of Northumberland has set out with an army to capture Mary.

The Marquis of Winchester brought the crown for me to try on. I did so with great reluctance. I can neither eat nor sleep. I am sick with anxiety. Guildford says I am foolish to worry. He is sure all will be well when his father has Mary under lock and key. Does he not realise the enormity of what we have done?

July 12 1553

The people have never liked Northumberland. They are muttering that Mary is the rightful Queen. They declare that they want the daughter not the niece. The Catholics among them are accusing him of persuading the dying King in the name of religion. I fear the future. If my father-in-law's plans go awry I could face a charge of High Treason.

Guildford was summoned by his father. When he returned he appeared to be ill at ease. After some hesitation he muttered that his father had exhorted him to demand the title of King. I will not have it so. I will do nothing to further the Earl's ambitious plans.

If Guildford were King, what then? Would I be found dead at the foot of a staircase or 'accidentally' drowned in the lake? In any event Guildford would find himself King in name only. His father would rule through him. This has been his purpose all along. I am seized with a feeling of dread. I shall never feel safe while John Dudley lives. These fears keep me from sleep. I lie awake filled with foreboding and overwhelmed by the gravity of my position.

July 14 1553

My father brought ill tidings. Northumberland's forces have been defeated. My father-in-law has misjudged the temper of the people. They consider he has tampered with the line of succession. He is universally hated. This may have influenced many to shout for Mary. He had reached Cambridge when he heard that his venture had failed.

My father tore down my banners and told me I must put off the royal robes and return to private life. My heart is full of thankfulness. I told him I took them off far more willingly than I ever put them on. Out of obedience to my parents I have grievously sinned. Now I willingly relinquish the crown.

I asked him if I could go home. He did not answer. Later I discovered he has changed sides to save his own skin. He has proclaimed Mary Queen at Cheapside to convince her of his loyalty. He has abandoned me.

Northumberland also tried to save himself by proclaiming Mary Queen but he had left it too late and he was taken prisoner.

Sir John Brydges told me the Council met at Baynard's Castle and pronounced Northumberland a traitor and Mary Queen. Guildford and I are under arrest.

July 15 1553

Mary and Elizabeth met at Wanstead and rode into London today in triumph. The people cheered them. Northumberland is in the Beauchamp Tower with Guildford and his other sons, John, Ambrose and Robert. Guildford wept when they came for him. I could not but feel pity for him. He is not to be blamed for his father's reckless schemes. We are both victims of that man's ambition. What will become of us now? My heart is heavy.

July 16 1553

Today is the day of Edward's funeral. I have not been allowed to attend. The funeral was held according to Protestant rites as he would have wished. Mary will not be pleased.

I have been thinking about Edward all day. How could he have been persuaded to pass over his sisters in favour of me? Well he knew his father's wishes, yet he flouted them. Northumberland has done this. He is overpowering and dictatorial and Edward was so weak and ill. It must have been easy to influence him for I know he desired above all that England should remain Protestant. He told me he wanted our country to hold to the faith of God as revealed in the Scriptures.

I cannot bring myself to lay blame at his door. I always found him good and kind and I know he loved me well. Dear Edward. Now he is at peace and free from all his suffering.

July 19 1553

I was sad when I learned today that John Cheke has been arrested for supporting me. He was always an ardent Protestant.

I have been moved to a house on the Green. It is quite comfortable and belongs to a man named Partridge.

Mary made a triumphal entry into the Tower today, accompanied by Elizabeth. She has been proclaimed Queen all over London. Her first act on entering the Tower was to send for three prisoners, the old Duke of Norfolk, Stephen Gardiner and Edward Courtenay, all staunch Catholics, imprisoned for their faith. She told them that they were now free men, and their estates restored to them.

I feel great relief that the farce is now over. I have nothing but contempt for my father, who has abandoned me to my fate and saved his own skin.

July 20 1553

Sir John Brydges has been very kind to me. He keeps me informed of all that is happening. He believes that Mary will hold nought against me. She has ordered a Requiem Mass to be said for Edward's soul and Bishop Gardiner will perform it. The Mass is being restored all over England. Whatever befalls I shall never forsake the Protestant Faith.

August 19 1553

Sir John brought me good news. Phoebe is to be allowed to join me. I am allowed two other female attendants and a page. I am content. I have my books and my journal and all the writing materials I need. I also have my Greek Testament and my prayer book. I am to be allowed ninety-three shillings a week, which is ample for my needs.

Sometimes I have dinner with the gentleman gaoler Partridge and his wife. Sir John lets me walk in his garden. Everyone is very kind. Sir John thinks that Guildford and I will be pardoned, albeit there will have to be a trial first.

I shall be glad to have Phoebe with me again.

August 22 1553

Today my father-in-law the Duke of Northumberland went to the block. I feel no pity for him. I think of all that has come about because of his ambition. His four sons are in the Tower and I am a prisoner. I wonder what Guildford is thinking this day. I have had no message from him, for they are kept in strict confinement.

Thousands of spectators gathered on Tower Hill to witness the execution of the Duke. He has denied the truth of the Protestant Faith. At the end he professed to have been converted to the Roman Catholic Faith, but this did not save him.

Some men are condemned unjustly but this man deserved to die.

September 4 1553

Phoebe has heard a rumour that Mary may marry Lord Courtenay. He is a suitable candidate being a Plantagenet, and very handsome to boot. Simon Renard the Spanish Ambassador, is urging Mary to marry Philip of Spain. This marriage would not be popular with the people. They mislike foreigners and they fear the consequences of such a match. The prospect of the flames at Smithfield strikes fear into the hearts of all Protestants, as well it might. Mayhap Mary will choose Courtenay. Since she released him from prison they are constantly in each other's company.

September 19 1553

I have written a letter to Mary. I told her that I never wanted the crown. I reminded her that Edward had just died and I was desolate. When they told me I was to be Queen I could scarcely take it in. I explained how I tried to protest, but they would not listen. I ended by saying that obedience to my father has brought me to where I now am and he has brought me to most miserable calamity by his exceeding ambition.

October 6 1553

Today I am sixteen years old. It has been a happy day. I have received gifts from Sir John Brydges and his wife and from Partridge, Phoebe and my ladies. Sir John is just like a father to me. I have grown very fond of him. Sometimes I speak to him of the uncertainty of my future and of my fears, and he reassures me. I count him as one of my blessings.

November 30 1553

Today is the day of Mary's coronation. She has not replied to the letter which I sent her in September. She sent her chaplain Feckenham to me, to try to convert me to the Roman Catholic religion. He came several times. I told him I shall never give up the Protestant Faith.

We had many discussions but he could not sway me. I told him I believe that faith alone saves. Men come to God if they believe in Him, and not by the Church. We parted with mutual respect.

December 3 1553

Phoebe has had letters from her family. She tells me that Sir Peter Carew has been going from town to town putting the people of Devon against the Spanish marriage. He tells of sailors who come into Devon ports who talk of the horrors of the Inquisition. He was summoned to London but he disappeared and his disappearance seems to have quelled the unrest in Devon.

Edward Courtenay, who was disappointed at being rejected by Mary, was at first suspected of being implicated. He allayed the suspicions of the Council by alerting them to the dangers of the situation in Devon.

January 25 1554

Christmas passed quietly. I remained in bed with a chill. Phoebe was such a comfort. She brought me possets and has nursed me so well that I am now almost recovered.

Mary has announced that she is to marry Philip of Spain. Sir Thomas Wyatt has raised the standard at Maidstone and is preparing to march on London. Both he and Edward Courtenay are against the Spanish marriage. Each has his reasons. Courtenay is piqued because he has been set aside in favour of Philip. Wyatt, who is fiercely Protestant, fears that England will return to Catholicism. He has described Spain as 'the evil spider of the world, looking to spread a web over England.'

February 6 1554

Sir John Brydges came to me with a grave countenance. Sir Thomas Wyatt has marched on London with four thousand men. Mary went in haste to the Guildhall and called upon the people to defend the city. When Wyatt reached Ludgate he was met by the Queen's men. He tried to retreat but it was too late. He surrendered at Temple Bar and is being brought to the Tower.

It seems he has conspired with Edward Courtenay and my father, the Duke of Suffolk. All three have been arrested. Courtenay has been restored to his Earldom of Devon, but when he saw there was no hope of marriage with Mary he rashly joined Wyatt. He has now confessed all to Gardiner and betrayed his two confederates, having first obtained a promise that he should not be beheaded. Consequently he has been sent into exile and is said to be somewhere in Italy.

Elizabeth is under suspicion. Wyatt had written to her but she is shrewd and she did not answer his letters. This may save her. When questioned she denied all knowledge of the rising and refused to become involved.

February 8 1554

Phoebe came to me in great distress. She was there when Wyatt was brought to the Tower today. She heard Sir John shouting at him that through his folly he has put my life in danger.

How can this be? I knew nothing of the rebellion. Surely Mary cannot believe that I was involved. Yet in truth my father was one of them. He too has been brought to the Tower. I care not for that, he has betrayed me a second time. I care not what becomes of him now.

February 9 1554

I had dinner with Sir John and Lady Brydges. They treat me as an honoured guest, with respect and deference and not as a prisoner. We were joined by Partridge who said little and looked very solemn. Sir John says I must not worry. He is sure Mary will not blame me for the events of the past months. Indeed I hope he is not mistaken. Yet I am fearful and I am aware of a heaviness of spirit which will not leave me. Phoebe too is quiet and this is not like her for she was ever a chatterbox.

The air is heavy as though a storm is about to break. God grant us a fair night's sleep and a good tidings on the morrow.

February 10 1554

We are to die, Guildford and I. Mary was reluctant to agree to our deaths but the Council has persuaded her that there will always be Protestant uprisings while we live. The Spanish ambassador has been urging her to this decision ever since the Wyatt rebellion. Obedience to my parents has brought me to this pass. Ambitious men sought power through my marriage, my father, Guildford's father and Thomas Wyatt. All three have played a part in bringing me to this end.

God knows I had no wish to be Queen. All I ever wanted was a quiet life, and my books, and the companionship of those I love. I had a brother and a sister who both died in infancy. That was the will of God. My death is by the will of unjust men. God and posterity will show me favour.

Edward and Katharine, the two I loved most in the world have gone on before. I believe I shall see them again.

I asked Sir John how Guildford was faring. He said he was very despondent and wept often. He has asked permission to see me to say farewell. I cannot see him. It will serve no purpose and will only unnerve us both. I have written to him. I told him we shall shortly behold each other in a better place.

February 12 1554

I have put on a black dress. Yesterday four matrons came to examine me to ensure that I was not pregnant. I have sent my Greek Testament to my sister Catherine. I have given Phoebe the silver cross and chain which dear Edward gave me seven years ago. I have sent her home to Devonshire. I cannot bear to see her distress. To Sir John Brydges, who has been so kind to me, I have sent some books.

They told me Guildford was to die first. I stood at the window and watched him walk weeping to Tower Hill. I thought he might turn and see me there, but he walked with head bent and shoulders bowed. I stood there waiting until his body was brought back in a handcart. O Guildford!

A scaffold has been erected over against the White Tower. Soon it will be my turn. Mary's chaplain Feckenham is to walk with me. He asked permission and I could not refuse, for he has been very kind, though he failed in his attempts to turn me from the Protestant Faith. He told me Mary would have spared my life if I had become a Roman Catholic. I replied that it was not my desire to prolong my days. I have no fear of death. If her Majesty wishes it, then I willingly undergo it.

I thank God I die a true Protestant.

They are coming for me now.

I am ready.

ENDS

At eight of the clock in the morning of February 12th, 1554 Lady Jane Grey was beheaded on Tower Green. Her body was interred in the nearby church of St Peter ad Vincula. She was sixteen years old.

Bibliography

Tower of London	Christopher Hibbert
The Tower of London in the History of the Nation	A.L. Rowse
A History of England	Keith Fielding
History of the Diocese of Exeter	Rev. R.J.E. Boggis MA BD
England in Tudor Times	L.F. Salzman MA FSA
History of England	J.A. Froude
British History	John Wade
Lives of the Queens of England	Agnes Strickland
The Tudor Age	J.A. Williamson
The Earlier Tudors	J.D. Mackie
The Elizabethans at Home	Elizabeth Burton
Sir Thomas More	Richard Marius
England under the Tudors	G.R. Elton
The England of Elizabeth	A.L. Rowse
The Wives of Henry the Eighth	Martin Hume
Henry the Eighth	Robert Lacey